Rainbow The Unicorn

Written by
David Seer

Illustrated by
Johanna Zverzina

Dedication

To those who believed in me, thank you.

And a big thanks to all those who put their love and energy into creating this magical book.

What a wonderful world it is when dreams do come true!

This Book Belongs to:

Published in association with Bear With Us Productions

©2020 David Seer

The right of David Seer as the author of this work has been asserted by his in accordance with the Copyright Designs and Patents Act 1988.

All rights reserved, including the right of reproduction in whole or part in any form.

Rainbow The Unicorn

Written by
David Seer

Illustrated by
Johanna Zverzina

What happens when dreams come true?

Zoey and her pet unicorn, Rainbow, are about to find out!

Rainbow is a really, REALLY special unicorn;
he is magic!

Wherever Rainbow goes, he leaves lots of color behind…
and lots of giggles too! He cheers everyone up with happy colors in their eyes.

Zoey and Rainbow have lots of fun together. When they play, they are always happy and the world seems better.

Rainbow's favorite treats are color sparkles!
But when Zoey gives them to him, he goes crazy silly!

First his eyes start to sparkle, then his unicorn horn sings, until his pearly-swirly horn sprinkles magic colors over everything!

And…

RAINBOW CAN FLY!

And make RAINBOWS in the sky!

Zoey loves riding on his back as they fly.

"Wee! Look at us! We're making a giggly, glittering rainbow-fest!" she joyfully cries.

"Uh-oh!" says Zoey. "Today I gave Rainbow too many color sparkles and he went crazy wild." Zoey peers into her room - it's a big mess! Rainbows are everywhere, on the floor and walls...
and even on her bed!

"Oops! There are some unicorn poopies on the rug!" Zoey giggles. "Pee-uww!" Zoey begins tidying up, hoping she's not in trouble. She mumbles, "Gee-wiz, it's going to take a long time to clean up my pet's mess. Wait a second, Rainbow!" Zoey shouts, "Come here right now and help me tidy up!"

There is no reply. She looks out of the window and listens... all is quiet.

Oh no! Rainbow has galloped away without Zoey! She's so sad.

"Rainbow! Rainbow! I need to find my Rainbow so I can be happy again!" Zoey cries as she searches everywhere.

"Please come back!"

She looks into the sky, with tears in her eyes.

"Wait! I see a rainbow.
That means my unicorn is out there somewhere, spreading fun and color!" Zoey says.

Zoey hopes nobody else is riding him.
"He is MY unicorn and makes me happy!"

Zoey imagines someone else having fun riding on his back and giggling. She wipes away her tears and takes a deep breath...

"I have to find him! I have to be brave, brave,
brave and have this adventure on my own."

How can Zoey be happy without Rainbow? So off she runs, as fast as she can, chasing rainbows in the sky.

A colorful puppy runs towards Zoey. "Hey, Spot!" she says, noticing his spots are rainbow-colored! "You've been rainbowed! Does that mean you've seen my unicorn?"

"I have," Spot smiles.
"He rainbowed my spots!"

"Do you know where he is?" Zoey pleads,
"I miss him so much."

"Don't be upset." Spot licks her and they giggle. Zoey tickles him and he licks her again until they fall around laughing together. Spot does the happy shakes, making his ears go flappity-flap and his color spots go hoppity-hop!

"Spot, you're so funny! But we have to find Rainbow." Zoey grins.

"OK," Spot barks. "Thank you for making me laugh, I've not laughed so much in a long time! Anyway, I didn't notice which way your wacky pet went, I was too busy counting my spotty color-fest! Grrr, he's such a pest!"

Spot sniffs the air. "Woof! Maybe he went that way?"

Spot and Zoey begin to search. High above,
another rainbow's in the sky.

"Look! I think we're getting closer!" Zoey tells Spot.

"Hisss!" A giant lizard sitting on a rock makes them jump.
"Your unicorn just went past, galloping across the sky very fast.
I don't know if you'll catch up, even with the help of Pup!"

"Oh no," Zoey feels sad, but notices lots of colors around the
lizard's eyes. "Hoo-boy!" Did he rainbow you too?"

"He did indeed! Do you like it?" Lizard replies.

"You look amazing!"
Zoey tells him. She feels good inside as the lizard smiles.

"Nobody has complimented me in a long time!" He says,
"If you want to find your unicorn, you need to go to the beach."

"Thank you!" Zoey shouts as she and Spot hurry to the sea.

At the beach what a cheery, merry sight meets their eyes! There are shiny shells on the sand below and a rainbow above in sparkly skies.

A family of sea turtles are making their way to the sea. "Excuse me!" Zoey calls,

"Have you seen my pet unicorn?"

"I'm sorry, no," Mummy turtle replies.

Zoey sighs, wishing she could find Rainbow. But before she and Spot look elsewhere, they help the baby sea turtles to get to the ocean.

"Thank you for your help!" the happy mummy says.

"You're so very kind! Nobody has been that kind to us in a long time."

Suddenly, dazzling dolphins jump up out of the waves, celebrating the baby turtles making it home.

They dance on their tails in a showy parade and shake their heads and sing.

"A-kee sqwee-ee! Thank you, little girl!" they call out to Zoey, while splashing around.
"You are very kind!"

"That's OK." Zoey smiles and her heart begins to glow.
It feels good to have helped.

"Thank you, lovely dolphins, you have put on quite a show, but I wonder, have you seen my lost pet, Rainbow?"

"Of course! To find your unicorn ask the fish, they saw him last! C'mon, follow us!"

Zoey soon finds fish splashing in the water and gasps with delight. The fish are a wonderful rainbowed sight!

"Did my pet unicorn rainbow you too?" Zoey asks.

"He did." Several fish nod.

"Yup! blub-blub!" says another.

Zoey watches them swimming and making beautiful patterns with their colors. She feels her sadness ebb away and happiness build up.

But...
"I still haven't found Rainbow," Zoey says.
"I don't know where to look?"

"Go find the Paradise Bird!"
one helpful fish says, blowing bubbles.

Spot's ears perk up. "Hey! I know where to look for the Paradise Bird! Woof!"

Spot and Zoey skip off the beach and run across green fields full of flowers.

They hear a beautiful song and follow it to the Paradise Bird. As the bird flutters in the sky, her sweet song sounds like an angel's sigh.

"There are rainbow colors here, there and everywhere!" Zoey says, noticing the glowing skies. "That must mean my Rainbow is very near!

"Hello, Zoey!" the Paradise Bird sings. "I'm glad you've come this way; you have made so many people happy today."

"I have?" Zoey asks.

"You made Spot giggle and laugh more than ever before.
You complimented Lizard which he'll remember for ever more.
Then you helped the baby turtles get home safe and sound.
And finally, you made happy... the most important person all around."

"Who?" Zoey wonders aloud.

"You!" Paradise Bird sings.

"Me?" Zoey questions. "Yes, you! Today you were nervous about having an adventure without Rainbow. You were worried you wouldn't be happy without him, but you have been! Whilst Rainbow spread his colors and love for miles, you helped others be happy and wear big smiles!"

A joyful Paradise Bird sings and Zoey joins in.

*"Rainbow, Rainbow the unicorn is magical colorful fun.
Teaching lessons about every color under the sun!
Today I learned to shine bright and have a happy heart,
Realizing happiness comes from within, that's where it starts!
Unicorns are a magical and mystical race, but Rainbow and me TOGETHER... make the whole world a happier place!
Yea, Rainbow!"*

Zoey dances with the Paradise Bird as they sing. A feather falls from her wing and lands in her hair. Zoey has a warm glowing heart and can't believe how happy she feels.

"You've learned an important lesson today, it's time that you caught that unicorn, so be on your way."

"My way?" Zoey stops dancing. "But I don't know where he is."

"I think you do." The Paradise Bird winks. "Feel the happiness inside and it will guide you to him."

Zoey thinks about how she feels. She's made others smile. She's been on an adventure on her own. She's feeling happy inside...

As the happiness within Zoey grows, the biggest, most colorful rainbow she has ever seen appears.

And right in the middle of it is...

"RAINBOW!"

Spot and Zoey run towards him, feeling excited. Lots of rainbowed animals cheer.

Zoey is SO happy she could BURST!

"Rainbow!" she calls to him.

"My lovely pet! I'm coming to get you! Your colors have brightened up so many animals' days, in lots of sparkly, colorful ways! And I learned I can bring happiness too!"

She can't wait to tell Rainbow all about her day.
She has to get closer, he just has to stay.

As they get nearer, Rainbow's pearly-swirly unicorn horn sparkles brightly and they hear its musical sound.

"Rainbow, I've missed you so much, but I also had fun, just wait until I tell you about everyone! You'll not believe the things that I have to say, about all the things that I've done today!"

In a flash, Rainbow whooshes out of the sky and lands on the colorful grass, they're together again at last. Zoey wraps her arms around Rainbow. "I'm so happy I've found you,
I missed you a lot!"

"I'm sorry I ran away," Rainbow says, hugging Zoey back.
"I guess I got too excited after having lots of sparkly treats."

Hugging her unicorn is the best feeling in the world.
But the sun is setting and the stars are beginning to sparkle.
It's time for Zoey and Rainbow to go home.

As Rainbow and Zoey curl up in bed that night, she tells him all about her adventure. About rolling around with Spot. About making the lizard feel good with the words she used. About helping the turtles get to safety.

"I did it all on my own. I made others happy by being me," Zoey says. "And that made me happy too."

"You are very special." Rainbow smiles.
"You can make people happy without magic."

"Tomorrow, we can have more adventures together!" she exclaims. Zoey closes her eyes and dreams about all the things she could do with Rainbow…

Like flying and playing chase!
Fun and games and lots of happiness!

In the morning it all feels hazy, a bit of a dream. Had it really happened, all those things that she'd seen?

"Are you magical? Can it be true?" Zoey whispers to Rainbow. "Did I go on an adventure looking for you?"

Zoey hurries downstairs for breakfast,
Rainbow clutched in her hands.

And that's when she notices the feather caught in her hair.
The one which fell from the Paradise Bird.

Zoey looks at Rainbow and is sure he winks at her.

"What a wonder you are, I'm so glad to have you," Zoey says.

She gives Rainbow a big hug full of love.

And that is how Zoey came to find out...

    What a wonderful world it is,
    when dreams come true.

          The End.

ACTIVITIES AND "HIDDEN GEMS" GAMES!

Join Rainbow's FAN CLUB!
You want answers! He's got answers;
"I will answer all my fans one rainbowy day!
I'm Rainbow the Unicorn!"

Wow! That sure was some colorful rainbow adventure Zoey
went on to find her unicorn!
Want more? Go to his website **www.goldenagedream.com**
and join the Rainbow the Unicorn FAN CLUB! Become a member!
You will find more Activities and clues and answers to **"Hidden Gems"**

ACTIVITY QUESTIONS:

Do you think Zoey felt her lost unicorn would ever be found?

Why did Zoey feel she could NOT let her wild pet be truly free?

Wasn't there alot of colors?
- What were all the colors "Rainbow" her pet unicorn made?
- Are they the same colors as the rainbow? Can you name them?
- Do you think colors can resemble emotions?
- Red when angry? Yellow when happy?

What did Zoey learn about manners on her adventure?

What was your favorite part? Was it riding Rainbow in the sky up to the stars?

Do you think that unicorns can do that?
What else can they do? Can you draw one?

Can you write a story or draw a picture? Full of fun and imagination from your mind and dreams? What was the best adventure or dream you ever had?

SEND your answers to the "Rainbow the Unicorn FAN CLUB."

DID YOU FIND THE HIDDEN GEMS OR "EASTER EGG" CLUES?

Starfish, stars, dreamcatcher, easter egg & more! HIDDEN GEMS-- secrets reveal clues that unlock more games, puzzles and prizes... on the Mysterious Unicorn Treasure Map. Find out about unicorn legend & The Land Of Unicornia. Want to learn more? Just go to the website!

So SIGN UP for more and become a club member!
FREE to join.

We'll send you invites to get free stuff; puzzles, mazes, coloring pages and book discounts! And for contest winners, win t-shirts to toys.

Are you ready?
Get your treasure map and discover a treasure trove of prizes!
Join the Rainbow the Unicorn FAN CLUB!

www.goldenagedream.com

Made in the USA
Monee, IL
22 December 2020